Hooray for Halloween!

By Diane Wright Landolf • Illustrated by Karen Wolcott

Cover photography by Joe Dias, Shirley Ushirogata, Bill Coutts, Greg Roccia, Lisa Collins, and Judy Tsuno

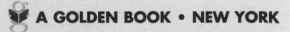 **A GOLDEN BOOK • NEW YORK**

BARBIE and associated trademarks and trade dress are owned by, and used under license from, Mattel, Inc. Copyright © 2004 Mattel, Inc. All Rights Reserved. Published in the United States by Golden Books, an imprint of Random House Children's Books, a division of Random House, Inc., New York, and simultaneously in Canada by Random House of Canada Limited, Toronto. No part of this book may be reproduced or copied in any form without written permission from the copyright owner. Golden Books, A Golden Book, and the G colophon are registered trademarks of Random House, Inc. Library of Congress Control Number: 2003105374   ISBN: 0-375-82757-9 www.goldenbooks.com   Printed in the United States of America   10 9 8 7 6 5 4 3 2

"We have so much to do for our Halloween party," Barbie says to her sister Kelly. "Let's put out the candy, decorate the house, and set up the games. We invited a lot of friends, so I really want it to be special."

"First, let's put on our costumes!" Barbie says. She zips on an orange-and-black-striped suit. Then she puts on ears and whiskers. Barbie is dressed as a tiger this Halloween!

PARTY TIME!

"I want to be a fairy," Kelly says.

"Okay," Barbie says. "Let's see what we can find in your closet."

Barbie helps Kelly pick out a dress. "This one would be perfect," Barbie says.

Then Barbie makes fairy wings for Kelly.
"There!" says Barbie. "Come on, little fairy,
we've got to decorate the living room."

"I'll put this creepy skeleton in the corner," Barbie says, "and stick cobwebs and spiders everywhere."
Then Barbie hangs up streamers and balloons. Kelly helps out by handing her the tape.

Barbie and Kelly go to the kitchen to get the Halloween treats. They come back with bags of candy.

"Let's put treats out all around the room," Barbie says. Kelly helps pour candy corn into bowls.

"These Halloween cookies came out great!" says Barbie as she puts the cookies on a tray. "Thanks for helping me make them, Kelly."

"May I have one now, or do I have to wait for the party?" asks Kelly.

"You may take one," Barbie says with a smile. "But just one."

Now it's time to set up Barbie's favorite Halloween game—bobbing for apples! Barbie fills a tub with water, and Kelly puts in the apples.

"Can I try bobbing for an apple?" Kelly asks.

"Sure," says Barbie.

Kelly dips her face into the water, trying to bite an apple. After a few seconds, she comes up with a nice red one!

"Good job, Kelly," says Barbie.

Barbie has one more thing to do before the party.
She can't forget the most important decoration of
all—the jack-o'-lantern!

Barbie picks up the carved pumpkin and puts a light inside. "I think this is the scariest jack-o'-lantern we've ever made!" she says as she takes it out the front door.

As Barbie walks back into the house, the living room
lights suddenly go out!

"What happened?" asks Kelly.

Then they hear a strange noise. *Ree-aw!*

"What was that?" Kelly asks.

"I don't know," says Barbie, reaching for Kelly's hand,
"but let's go and get a candle from the kitchen."

Barbie and Kelly tiptoe to the kitchen and turn
on the lights.

They look all around, but they don't see anything
that could have made the spooky sound.

Suddenly, they hear the noise again! *Ree-aw!*
"That sounded like it came from the living room," says Barbie. She finds a candle in the kitchen drawer and lights it. "Come on!" she says.

Barbie and Kelly rush into the living room and find . . .
Whiskers, their cat, playing with the streamers! He wants
to join in the Halloween fun!

"Oh, Whiskers!" says Barbie, laughing. "Look, he must
have pulled the lamp cord while he was playing, and turned
off the lights."

"Whiskers, you scared us!" says Kelly.

"Well, it wouldn't be Halloween without a good scare," Barbie says.

Ding-dong!

"That must be the first party guest," says Barbie, walking to the door. "Now that we've gotten our Halloween scare out of the way, let's have fun!"